Billy & Rose

JUST THE WAY
THEY ARE

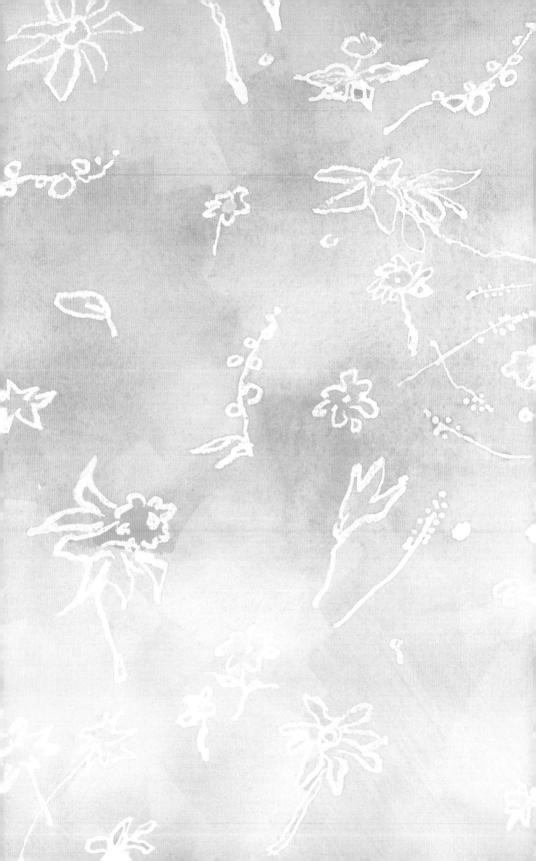

Billy & Rose

JUST THE WAY
THEY ARE

Amy Hest

illustrated by
Kady MacDonald Denton

CANDLEWICK PRESS

For Lev, Rosie, and Frieda
Just the way they are
Love, Nonnie
AH

For B.B.
KMD

Text copyright © 2023 by Amy Hest
Illustrations copyright © 2023 by Kady MacDonald Denton

First edition 2023
Library of Congress Catalog Card Number 2022922912
ISBN 978-1-5362-1420-8

23 24 25 26 27 28 CCP 10 9 8 7 6 5 4 3 2 1

Printed in Shenzhen, Guangdong, China

This book was typeset in Utopia.
The illustrations were done in watercolor and ink.

Candlewick Press
99 Dover Street
Somerville, Massachusetts 02144

www.candlewick.com

CONTENTS

Books

Billy and Rose are having a serious discussion. The subject is books.

"I like tall blue books," says Rose. "Tall blue books are the best."

"Fat red books. Those are the best," says Billy.

Rose leans against a tree with her tall blue book. Slowly, she turns the pages.

Billy leans close. He looks at the pictures in Rose's tall blue book.

When the story is over, Billy is sad. He is mellow.

"Why are you sad?" asks Rose.

"Because the story is over." Billy sighs a big sigh, then opens his book. One by one, he turns the pages.

Rose leans close. She looks at the pictures in Billy's fat red book.

When the story is over, Rose is sad. She is mellow.

"It's over," says Rose with a sigh. "Now what?"

"We'll think of something," says Billy.

"Oh, yes," agrees Rose. "Something."

They think for a while. And think for a
while.

And walk around the yard with their
books.

And sit in the grass with their books.

They lean against a tree with two best
books. Then Billy looks at Rose, and Rose
looks at Billy.

"Again?" whispers Rose.

"Again," whispers Billy.

Together, they turn the pages of their books.

Together, and one by one, they look at
all the pictures in two best books. Again and
again and again.

And they never run out of stories.

Rain

Billy and Rose are having a serious discussion. The subject is rain.

"Let's go for a walk," says Rose. "I'll take my umbrella. In case it rains."

"It's not going to rain," Billy tells Rose.

"Nevertheless," says Rose, "one must be prepared."

Billy and Rose walk into the lane. On either side of the lane, flowers bloom. So many yellow flowers. Above the lane, the sky is blue.

Rose opens her purple umbrella.

"Announcing," she says. "I'm ready for rain!"

"It's not going to rain," Billy tells Rose. He
skips ahead.

Rose skips up to Billy. She looks at the sky. The blue, blue sky. "We have to *hope* it rains," Rose says.

"But I don't hope it rains," Billy tells Rose. Rose starts to cry.

"Why are you crying?" Billy asks Rose.

"Because the sun is bright, the sky is blue, and I want to walk in the rain with you. Under my purple umbrella," sniffs Rose.

Now Billy starts to cry.

"Why are you crying?" asks Rose.

"Because you always have good ideas,"
Billy tells Rose.

"Yes," agrees Rose. "I do."

Just then, the sun goes away and the sky turns gray. Then dark gray.

And darker.

"Announcing," says Billy. "It's going to rain!"

Together, Billy and Rose open the umbrella. And together they walk in the rain, under the purple umbrella.

Hair

Billy and Rose are having a serious discussion. The subject is hair.

"I am having a bad hair day," Billy tells Rose. "Look at me, Rose. Look at my hair. Sticking up here, sticking out there!"

Rose takes a good long look at Billy's hair.

"Well?" Billy asks. "What do you think?"

"I think you are having a bad hair day,"
says Rose.

"How could you say that!" Billy says.

"*You* said it first," says Rose. "I only said what *you* said first."

"And I only said it so you would say *I like you just the way you are,*" Billy explains to Rose.

"That's ridiculous," says Rose. "Of course I like you just the way you are!"

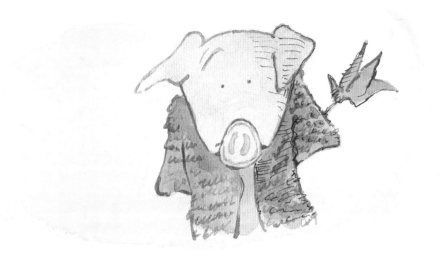

"Even when my hair sticks up and out?"
"Even then," says Rose.

"Really, truly?" Billy asks.

"Really, truly," says Rose. "I like you just the way you are."

"And I like you just the way you are," Billy tells Rose.

"Good," she says, then hands him a comb.

"Now comb your hair, Billy," whispers Rose.

And he does.

STORY 4

Cupcakes

Billy and Rose are having a serious discussion. The subject is cupcakes.

"I want a cupcake today for my birthday," says Rose.

"But it isn't your birthday," says Billy.

"That's not the point", says Rose. "The point is chocolate. My cupcake will be chocolate. I'll bake it myself, and the candles will be blue."

"I think not." Billy smiles at Rose.

"Vanilla's the way to go. With vanilla cream frosting and sprinkles. And yellow candles."

"I like chocolate." Rose smiles back.
"Chocolate, inside and out."

Billy shakes his head. "You should like what I like, Rose. Friends like the same thing."

"I do like what you like, Billy. Only, I like what I like more," says Rose. "My birthday, I choose."

"But it isn't your birthday," says Billy.

"That's not the point," Rose says with a sigh. "The point is goodbye, Billy."

"Fine!" Billy frowns a big frown. "Then goodbye, Rose."

They both stomp off to their separate
homes.

Billy thinks about Rose. And birthdays.
And baking. And Rose.

Rose thinks about Billy. And birthdays.
And baking. And Billy.

A long time passes. (Much too long.) But when the time is right, Billy and Rose meet up in the yard. They each hold a silver box.

Rose gives her silver box to Billy. Inside, he finds a cupcake. Vanilla with vanilla cream frosting and sprinkles. The candles are yellow.

Billy gives his box to Rose. The cupcake inside is chocolate, inside and out. The candles are blue. Rose starts to cry.

"Why are you crying?" asks Billy.

"Because it's not my birthday," sniffs Rose.

"That's not the point," says Billy. "The point is cupcakes."

"You're right." Rose sniffs some more.
"The point is cupcakes."

As the sun sinks in the western sky, they lounge in the green, green grass, eating cupcakes. Because that's what friends do.